A CHRISTMAS CAROL

Louis Weber, C.E.O.
Publications International, Ltd.
7373 North Cicero Avenue
Lincolnwood, Illinois 60712

3rd Floor, 3 Princes Street, London W1R 7RA

www.pilbooks.com

Manufactured in China.

8 7 6 5 4 3 2 1

ISBN 0-7853-9383-8

A CHRISTMAS CAROL

Based on the story by Charles Dickens
Illustrated by Kathy Wilburn

 publications international, ltd.

Once upon a time, and on a Christmas Eve, Ebenezer Scrooge sat in his cold, bare office counting his money. Scrooge's clerk, Bob Cratchit, warmed himself over a tiny candle.

Cratchit cleared his throat. "Mr. Scrooge, sir," he said, "tomorrow is Christmas…."

"And I suppose you'll be wanting the day off," Scrooge snarled.

"Why, yes, sir. I'd like to spend Christmas with my family," said Cratchit.

"Christmas. Bah humbug, that's what I say!" Scrooge growled gruffly.

A knock at the office door announced a cheerful group of carolers. "Carolers. Bah humbug," grumbled Scrooge as he turned his back on them.

A little later, a second knock came from a kind man who was collecting money for the poor. "Charity. Bah humbug," scoffed Scrooge as he slammed the door in the man's face.

A third knock at the door was delivered by Scrooge's friendly young nephew, Fred.

"Hello, Uncle! I've come to invite you to Christmas dinner. Please come," Fred pleaded.

But "Bah humbug" was all that Scrooge had to say.

Later that evening, Scrooge went home. As he turned the key in the lock, the doorknocker changed into the face of his old partner, Jacob Marley.

Scrooge looked twice before muttering, "Humbug." But that night the ghost of Marley paid Scrooge a visit.

"I have come to warn you," moaned Marley's ghost. "When I was alive, I cared only about money, never about kindness or love. Now I walk the earth wearing these chains I created in life. If you do not change your ways, you will be like me. Therefore, tonight you will be visited by three ghosts."

Scrooge closed his eyes tight. When he opened them, Marley's ghost was gone. Scrooge went to bed.

Bong! The clock struck one, and Scrooge awoke suddenly. Feeling cold, he pulled his blankets around him. He sensed that there was a presence in the room other than his own. Much to his surprise, Scrooge saw a ghostly figure approaching him!

"Are you the spirit I was told would come?" asked Scrooge in a shaky voice.

"I am the Ghost of Christmas Past—your past," the spirit said in a gentle voice. "Come with me." Scrooge allowed the spirit to lead him away.

Scrooge found himself standing in a classroom. The place felt very familiar. A lone boy sat reading nearby.

"Why, that boy is me," said Scrooge. "I had been left behind by my classmates and my father. I spent a very lonely Christmas in this classroom that year."

Scrooge went over to the boy. He wiped a tear from his own eye, and remembered how alone he had felt.

"Come," said the spirit, "there is more to see."

"Do you recognize this place?" asked the spirit. Scrooge looked around and saw a large banquet hall filled with people, all enjoying a Christmas party.

"Why, of course! This was a party hosted by none other than good old Fezziwig. He was a wonderful boss," said Scrooge happily. "And it was a wonderful party."

"Indeed," said the spirit. "And now I have one more thing to show you."

Before them knelt a far more serious Scrooge than before. A woman spoke to him in a voice that was heavy with heartbreak. "I cannot marry you, Scrooge. You love your money more than me," she said.

"Take me away from here," Scrooge begged the spirit. "I cannot bear it." Instantly, Scrooge was in his own bed. He fell fast asleep.

Bong! Bong! The clock struck two. Scrooge woke in his room, but it didn't seem like his room. The walls glowed with the golden light from a warm fire in the fireplace. Filling the room with a jolly presence was a smiling giant with twinkling eyes.

"I am the Ghost of Christmas Present," said the giant.

"Spirit," said Scrooge, "I am ready to learn."

"Then touch my robe."

Scrooge did. Instantly he found himself on a bustling Christmastime street.

"Look in here," said the spirit, crouching down to peer into a frosty window. Scrooge looked through the window and saw Bob Cratchit with his family. Bob Cratchit held his son, Tiny Tim, whose little crutch leaned nearby. Every last Cratchit looked joyful, even though their dinner was no bounty. In fact, Scrooge thought it was the leanest dinner he had ever seen.

The family said a prayer of thanks, and then began to talk and laugh again. The look of love shone in all their eyes … especially poor Tiny Tim's.

"Spirit, what will happen to Tiny Tim?" asked Scrooge. The Ghost of Christmas Present did not answer.

Bong! Bong! Bong! The clock struck three. Scrooge woke yet again—this time to see a most terrifying spirit draped all in black from head to toe.

"Are you the Ghost of Christmas Yet to Come?" asked Scrooge. "You will show me things that have not yet happened?"

The spirit slowly raised an arm and pointed.

"Spirit, I fear you most ... but I wish to live a better life. I will go with you," said Scrooge.

Without a word, the spirit began walking. Scrooge followed and soon found himself on a snowy morning street.

The spirit pointed to villagers who were talking on the street. Scrooge listened.

"When did the old miser die?" asked one.

"Yesterday. Finally! It took him long enough!" Everyone laughed. Cruel cackles filled the air.

Scrooge understood why they laughed. "I don't want to be remembered this way," he said.

The spirit pointed again. Scrooge found
himself in an eerie, deserted graveyard. The
spirit pointed to a grave overgrown with
weeds. Scrooge knew at once that no one
must care about the grave enough to look
after it. Scrooge brushed away some
snow and tangled vines. When
Scrooge saw his own name on
the stone, he cried, "Take
me away from here!"

Again, Scrooge found himself at Bob Cratchit's house. Cratchit held a child on each knee. This time their faces were full of sorrow. Tiny Tim's crutch and empty chair sat unused before the fireplace. No fire warmed the Cratchit house that day.

"Spirit, tell me this does not have to happen. I will change my ways. I will keep Christmas in my heart every day of the year," promised Ebenezer Scrooge.

Although he did not hear the clock strike again,
Scrooge woke to a beautiful Christmas morning.
A new feeling was welling up deep inside his heart.
He hurried to his window and called down
to a passing boy.

"Hurry to the butcher! Buy the fattest
goose! I will pay you well for your
trouble!" Scrooge said.

Next, Scrooge set out in his finest suit. He came upon the man who had asked for money for the poor.

"This is for our less fortunate friends," said Scrooge, handing him an envelope filled with money. The man was so shocked that he didn't know what to say!

Next Scrooge saw the carolers. He applauded them loudly, and even sang along!

Scrooge then paid a visit to his surprised nephew Fred. And what a visit! Scrooge came weighed down with gifts and treats and a "Happy Christmas" for all!

The very last visit Ebenezer Scrooge made that Christmas day was to the Cratchit home. He brought gifts and sweets and a goose as big as Tiny Tim. And that Christmas, Ebenezer Scrooge sat down with the Cratchit family to the biggest, best, and most joyful Christmas feast any of them had ever had. After a toast, Tiny Tim gave Scrooge a smile and said, "Merry Christmas … and bless us, every one!"

Bless Us,
Every One!